This igloo book belongs to:

.............................................................

# igloobooks

*Published in 2019*
*by Igloo Books Ltd*
*Cottage Farm*
*Sywell*
*NN6 0BJ*
*www.igloobooks.com*

*Written by Dee Hunt*
*Illustrated by Diane Le Feyer*

*Designed and edited by Lee Italiano*

*1219 003*
*4 6 8 10 9 7 5 3*
*ISBN 978-1-78670-594-5*

*Printed and manufactured in China*

*Dedicated to Nan*

# Poor Old Ted

igloobooks

Poor Old Ted
isn't wanted
any more.

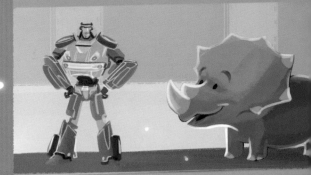

A long time ago
he was put
into a cot...

... when my grandson Lee was just a tot.

He was always waiting when...

... my grandson came to stay...

Ted's been
kissed and
cuddled...

... and **pushed**
down the bed...

... wheeled in a doll's pram...

... and **dropped** on his head.

Hours were spent, just Ted and Lee...

... talking of **adventure** and sipping tea.

Tireless Ted
never left
Lee's side...

... except when Teela gave him a ride.

One night,
as usual,
I tucked
Lee into
bed.

We had
a cuddle,
a kiss,
and I
handed
over
Ted.

"No thank you, Nan,"
Lee said quite loudly.

"I'm six years old now,"
he smiled so proudly.

"Big boys don't need toys to cuddle any more."

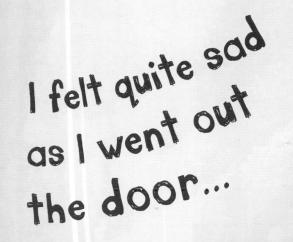

I felt quite sad
as I went out
the door...

... to see old Ted
lying on the floor.

I went to make the beds the very next day, when Lee and his sister had gone out to play.

Guess where I found poor unwanted Ted?

**Yes!**
All wrapped up in Lee's warm bed.

When questioned why
the change of heart
and why from
Ted he could
not part...

... with big
blue eyes
and a smile
he said...

..."I fink I'll wait till I'm seven instead!"